For my little sister Tessa

First published in the United Kingdom in 2014 by
Pavilion Children's Books
an imprint of Pavilion Books Company Limited
1 Gower Street
London WC1E 6HD

Design and layout © Pavilion Children's Books, 2014
Text and illustrations © Frann Preston-Gannon, 2014

The moral rights of the author and illustrator have
been asserted.

ISBN 9781843652939

A CIP catalogue record for this book
is available from the British Library

20 19 18 17 16 15 14
10 9 8 7 6 5 4 3 2 1

Reproduction by Mission Productions Ltd, Hong Kong
Printed and bound by 1010 Printing International Ltd, China

This book can be ordered directly from the publisher
online at www.pavilionbooks.com

Sloth Slept On

Frann Preston-Gannon

PAVILION

He wasn't like any other creature
we had ever found in the garden.

We asked him his name.
We asked what he
was doing up in our tree.

But there was no answer...
He was asleep.

MISSING!

please return to the zoo.

We had lots of questions.
So we set off to find some answers.

First we asked Dad what he thought.
But he was busy.

We looked in all the books we could find.
They were full of pictures and words
and places and things, but there was
nothing that looked like our new friend.

We knew he wasn't an elephant. He didn't have a trunk.
He wasn't a tiger either. He didn't have any stripes.
He wasn't a horse or a bear.

He let out a loud snore.
He was still asleep.

Perhaps he didn't belong in our garden at all.
Maybe he had travelled for a very long time,
from somewhere far away.

Maybe he was a ferocious pirate that
had been sailing the seas and was
sleepy from all his adventures.

He might even be a brave knight
who was exhausted from spending
all his time fighting dragons.

'He is not an elephant or a spaceman or a pirate or a knight!'

He is an animal called a SLOTH.

We learnt that our friend usually lives in the beautiful rainforests of Central and South America.

This sloth is a type called a three-toed sloth, who uses his strong grip to stay in the trees.

Sloths move veeeeery. v e e e e e r y slowly.

The sloth is a very sleepy animal. He can sleep hanging in a tree for up to 20 hours a day!

Sometimes a sloth lives in the same tree in the rainforest for years at a time.

The rainforest has all the things that a sloth likes to eat best, such as leaves, fruit, twigs and even bugs!

The rainforest sounded wonderful.
We decided there was only one thing for it.

We found a nice big box and used
all the stamps we could find.
We packed him some lovely leaves
to eat and toys for the journey.

MISSING!

If found please return to the zoo.

We were so happy the sloth had come
all the way from the rainforest to visit.

We would miss him lots but we were
glad that he would be waking up
back where he belonged.

Deep in the rainforest the sloth
finally stirred. He had been
having the most wonderful
sleep. He slowly lifted his head,
looked around and said...

POST

PLEASE SEND TO
THE RAINFOREST

'...Excuse me.
Which way is the Zoo?'

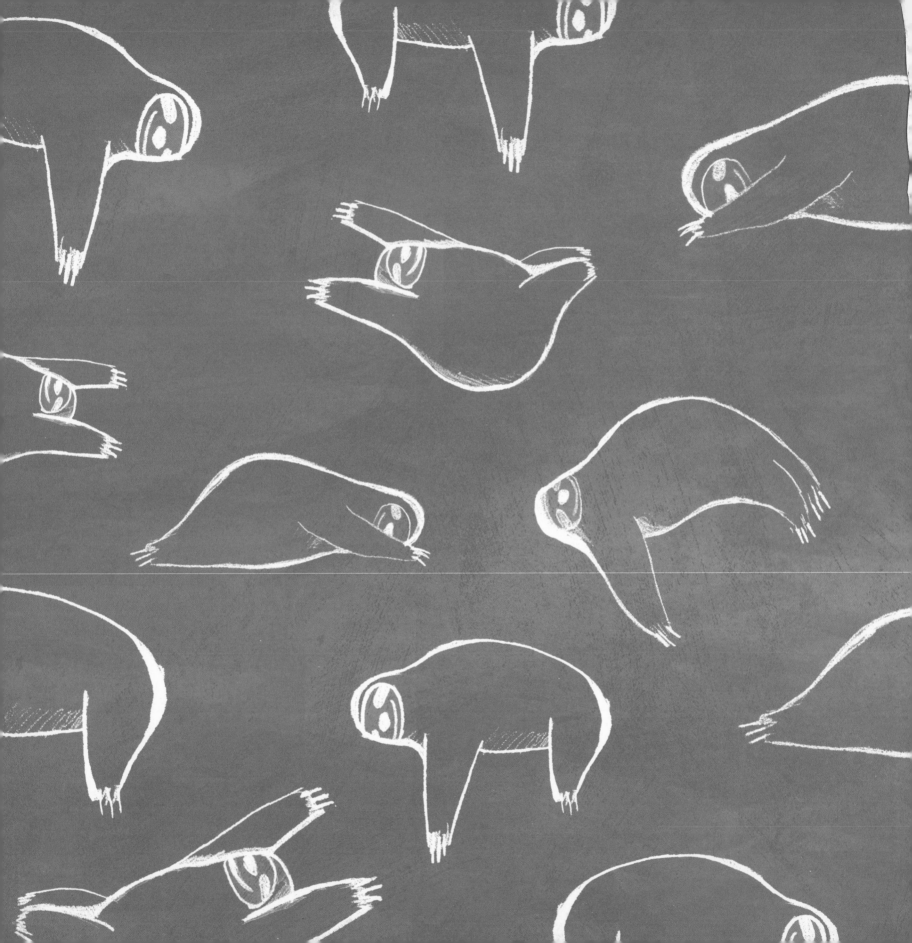